Tales Upchu Station

by Robert Gillman
Illustrated & Designed by Alan Ward

Five Wonderful Railway Stories

for Children

Railway Cat Creations

Tales of Upchurch Station
Written by Robert Gillman
Designed & Illustrated by Alan Ward

ISBN 978-0-9537406-3-5

Published by Railway Cat Creations
PO Box 299, Rainham, Essex, RM13 8XT

Printed in England by
BMK Printers, Dagenham

INTRODUCTION

Today's Heritage Railways belong to our children. We are merely custodians of something we hope, as parents and doting grandparents, to have developed, restored, cherished and promoted to the point of being able to hand over with pride and satisfaction in a job well done.

The joy of children, shaking with excitement, faces beaming at the numerous heritage steam railway events, is ample reward for the growing band of selfless volunteers who have made the heritage movement what it is today.

Over the years, Bob and I have been privileged to witness these events many times, and feel sure that the future is in very good hands.

The stories you are about to read, reflect in many ways a way of life that has gone, but never to be forgotten. Many seemingly old fashioned messages and values are evident throughout. Perhaps they *also* echo a hope for the future.

Alan Ward

CONTENTS:

TALES OF
UPCHURCH STATION

SIR HARRY HURRY'S DOZE

By Robert Gillman

Upchurch was a very sleepy town, not far from the countryside. At the top of the town was Upchurch station, which was just as sleepy, although sometimes it was a scene of great activity.

The station was a terminus, which meant that it was right at the end of the line, and the only thing beyond the station was a big depot, where all the trains went at night.

Upchurch was just the kind of place where everybody knew everybody else, which was sometimes quite a disadvantage when a secret had to be kept; and Sir Harry Hurry wished he could have kept his.

You see, Sir Harry Hurry was a very important man in the town. He busied himself running businesses here and businesses there, in all the towns along the railway line, and he prided himself on being very efficient.

He was a close friend of the Mayor and all the town councillors, and he was always in a hurry. In fact, all Sir Harry Hurry's friends just called him plain Sir Hurry.

At the station, everyone knew Sir Harry very well, particularly as he was always rushing and wanted to know everything that was going on.

He was always pestering Stanley the Station Master, wanting to know when he would be announcing the time the next train would be leaving.

He would also cause great consternation by marching into Stanley's office and using his 'phone to ring Sam the Signalman.

Sir Harry always wanted to be efficient, and didn't know what it was like to be patient.

He would always be telling Sam to wake up and make the signals green so that his train could go.

Now Sam may have been a bit slow, but he was always awake and made his signals green at exactly the right time.

On one particular day, Sir Harry had to go all the way to Bigtown. By special invitation, he had been asked to go to a banquet. All his friends at Bigtown had decided to honour him and he had a large trophy presented to him with his name engraved on it, thanking him for his work in Bigtown.

Normally, Sir Harry did not drink, but he *was* partial to a drop of ginger wine on special occasions. The evening passed extremely pleasantly, and all his friends kept topping up Sir Harry's glass.

At last it was time to go home and Sir Harry made his way contentedly to Bigtown station for his journey back to Upchurch.

The train to Upchurch was extremely comfortable, and Sir Harry settled down for a quiet doze on the way home; the ginger wine had gone straight to his head.

Meanwhile, Sam the Signalman had been quite busy, as late at night all the trains had to be put to bed. Sam felt quite ready for bed himself, but he had to wait for the last train from Bigtown to arrive.

At last it came chuffing into the station and the last few passengers stumbled off home to their beds. Sam picked up the 'phone and rang the shunter's cabin in the depot.

Sid the Shunter answered and Sam told him that the last train was coming down for him to put to bed.

Sam was very pleased to have finished his day's work and picked up his bag and tea can and made his way to the door of the signalbox.

He was just locking up for the night when the 'phone started ringing. The 'phone never rang at this time of night, and Sam just wanted to go home and see Betsy, his ginger cat.

Well, who do you think it was?
It was Sid the Shunter, and he was quite
agitated. "Sam, Sam - we've got somebody
still on the train."

"Who is it?" asked Sam.

"It's Sir Harry,
and he's sleeping like a baby!"

"Well, I'll be jiggered," said Sam. "You'll have to bring the train back out of the depot."

"Oh bother!" said Sid. "My bread pudding will be cold by the time I get back."

It was just about then that Sir Harry woke up and realised where he was. He felt extremely embarrassed that he had overslept and caused so much trouble.

When the train was shunted back to the station, Sir Harry quickly stumbled off to his big house in the middle of town.

He was so embarrassed that he vowed never to tell anyone at the station to hurry up again.

He promised Sid a big dish of hot bread pudding, and Sam's cat, Betsy, a plate of best salmon, if they would keep quiet about what had happened.

Both Sid and Sam promised not to say anything. It would be their secret.

Strangely enough, although Sid and Sam never spoke to anyone, everyone in the town seemed to know all about it, and smiled knowingly to each other as they passed by in the High Street.

Some would even stop and giggle, and then chat about the day the efficient Sir Harry Hurry dozed off and ended up in the depot.

You see, Upchurch was a place where it was very hard to keep a secret.

TALES OF
UPCHURCH STATION

SID THE SHUNTER'S SANDWICH
by Robert Gillman

Upchurch Station was right at the end of the railway line, which was why it was called a terminus.

Sometimes it was very quiet when all the trains had left, but at other times, things were very hectic, especially in the mornings.

This was because all the trains that had been put to bed at night in the depot, had to come out for the morning rush hour to take people to work in Bigtown and other places along the line.

A very important person who helped
to get the trains ready was Sid the Shunter.
He had to make sure the coaches were all in
the right order, and that each train had the
right number of coaches to suit the engine
that would be pulling them.

On this particular day, Sid had been late
leaving home. He had overslept, so he only
got to work at the depot just in time.

But just as he came in through the door of his shunter's cabin, he realised something. Horror of horrors, tragedy of tragedies: he had forgotten to bring his sandwiches.

"Drat and double drat," muttered Sid. "Now what am I to do?"

You see, Sid was a very good shunter and was respected by all the drivers and depot staff, but he did not work very well on an empty stomach.

All the drivers had noticed Sid was not paying full attention to his work, and if he wasn't careful, the coaches wouldn't be ready in time, and trains would be late.

Well now, things were beginning to look really bad, because even the passengers waiting patiently on the platform could hear the rumble, rumble, rumbling of Sid's empty stomach.

It was then that Derek the Engine Driver
made a decision. He called all the engine
drivers together and had a meeting.

"We can't carry on like this," said one of the other drivers. "Sid just doesn't work well on an empty stomach."

Suddenly, Derek had an idea. "Look, chaps," he said, "this is what we'll do," and he proceeded to tell the other drivers his plan.

After a lot of head shaking and nodding, they all trooped out to see Sid. They knew exactly where to find him, by listening for the rumbling sound of Sid's empty tummy.

"Hey, Sid!" shouted Derek. Sid looked up from his sad attempts to couple-up two coaches, and saw all the drivers walking across the tracks to meet him.

"Hey Sid, hold your hands out," urged Derek.

"What's all this?" muttered Sid.

"Look, just hold your hands out, will you?"

Almost in a daze, Sid did what he was told, and Derek promptly slapped a thick slice of bread and butter in each hand.

By now, all the drivers had formed an orderly line behind Derek. The next driver to come by Sid, laid two lettuce leaves on the slices of bread. The next driver followed with some sliced beetroot and a spring onion.

The next one put on half a boiled egg, and the one after that, a slice of ham.

So it went on, until the last driver had passed by a bewildered-looking Sid.

Just to finish off, Derek placed one of the slices of bread on top of the other and, grinning broadly, said, "Now Sid, eat that up and get some strength back, so we can all have our trains leaving on time."

Well, you've never before seen such a fat sandwich, and never before seen such a hungry man make it disappear so fast.

The transformation was immediate and nobody had seen Sid move quite so quickly, whizzing here and whizzing there, until all the trains were ready.

Just before the first train was about to leave, Sid grabbed Derek by the hand and thanked him for the food. "But won't *all* of *you* be hungry now?" he asked.

"Well," said Derek, "we knew that if we all gave you a little bit from our sandwiches, there would still be plenty for us, and enough for you."

"Well, I never!" said Sid. "I never had so many different things in a sandwich before, especially when the last driver spread jam on the lettuce!"

But of course Sid had been too hungry to care; and what did it matter, so long as the trains were ready on time, which - with a little help from his friends - they were.

TALES OF
UPCHURCH STATION

MRS FLOUNCE
GOES SHOPPING
by Robert Gillman

Now, as you know, Upchurch was a busy little town, right at the end of the railway line. Because of this, certain people were very important. One of these very important people was Mr Coombes.

Mr Coombes was very important because he had a shop. Not just any old shop, but a big shop, which sold practically everything.

Coombes Store was known as a department store because it had lots of different parts.

Mr Coombes was well respected in the town. He was carrying on the family business that his grandfather had started and his father had helped to develop.

Coombes Store was now the biggest shop in town and Mr Coombes was very proud of it, too. Because Coombes Store was so big, and it was near the railway, it had its very own siding, where all the great variety of things came in.

Three times a week, a goods train would pull its wagons into Coombes' siding, ready for the warehousemen to unload.
Now Coombes' right hand man, and the person who helped everything run smoothly, was Major Tucker.

Major Tucker had been an engineer when he was in the army and, as the general manager of Coombes Store, he ran it as if it were a clock.

This meant he insisted everything worked to a strict timetable, and all the staff in the departments had to follow his exact instructions. As you can imagine, this caused all sorts of problems with the staff, as they felt they were in the army, too.

Now, it so happened on this particular day that Coombes Store had a visitor.
The doors burst open and in waltzed Mrs Flounce. Major Tucker, who was standing just inside, went pale.

You see, Mrs Flounce was married to Colonel Flounce, who in his earlier life had been Major Tucker's commanding officer: a fact Mrs Flounce knew very well.
Major Tucker quietly braced himself for what was to come.

"Major Tucker," summoned Mrs Flounce, tossing back her head. "Major Tucker, you may recall that I ordered a certain item from you, two weeks ago. I have had neither sight nor sound from you regarding the matter since!"

Major Tucker's pale face became even paler.

"Dear me," he thought, "now, what was it? Furniture, cut glass crystal, cutlery, shoes, underwear?"

"Well, man, what have you to say?" persisted Mrs Flounce.

"If madam would kindly take a seat, I will establish what the precise situation is," said Major Tucker, trying to retain his composure and play for time.

Hurriedly, Major Tucker disappeard into the office to ask Mabel, the Order Clerk.

"It's not here yet, Sir," hissed Mabel, checking her order book.

Desperately, Major Tucker picked up the telephone and rang the depot at Bigtown. After a hurried conversation, he rushed out of the office to speak to Mrs Flounce.

"Well, Tucker?" she demanded, "where is it? Roland will not be pleased if there has been inefficiency!"

Major Tucker was never allowed to call Colonel Flounce 'Roland,' but he knew when he was in the firing line.

"Dear Mrs Flounce" he stammered, "I assure you it is on its way. Indeed, we deemed it of such importance, and we value your custom so highly, it is on the train at this precise moment."

"Harumph!" said Mrs Flounce, tossing her head back.

"It will be here within the hour," assured Major Tucker. "In the meantime, do come through and have some tea in my office."

Shortly afterwards, the 'phone rang for Major Tucker. It was Sid the Shunter.

"Major, I think you'd better come down," said Sid.

Major Tucker hurried down to Coombes' siding, to be confronted with Sid scratching his head. There in the siding was a goods train, but it had only one wagon - a huge covered affair that looked like it would hold a tank.

"Open it up, Sid," commanded Major Tucker.

So Sid duly opened the huge doors on the side of the wagon. As they peered inside, Sid commented, "Well, I never!"

For there, in the middle of the huge wagon floor, was a huge wooden crate.

"Come on Sid, open it up," said Major Tucker impatiently. Sid got out his big crowbar and gradually levered the lid off the crate. As they peered inside, all they could see was lots of straw.

Gradually, Sid managed to get most of the straw out of the way. "Well, I never," said Sid, for there in the middle of the huge crate, in the middle of the huge wagon,
was just a hat box!

Yes, a special train had been sent just to deliver the hat that Mrs Flounce had been waiting for.

"Well, I never," said Sid, again.

"You have to remember that Mrs Flounce is one of our best customers," said Major Tucker. With that, he hurried off, hopefully to put a smile on Mrs Flounce's face.......or the nearest thing to it, anyway.

In any case, Major Tucker was very relieved that he did not have to face the wrath of Roland, or Mrs Flounce, and it all ended happily.

Only Sid the Shunter was left wondering what the world had come to, sending special trains for hats!

"Well, I never,"
said Sid, scratching
his head.

TALES OF
UPCHURCH STATION

BETSY SAVES THE DAY
by
Robert Gillman

Derek the Engine Driver had been working at Upchurch for more years than he cared to remember. Everyone knew Derek and respected him for all the knowledge and experience he had gained since he had joined the railway. What Derek didn't know about the railway wasn't worth knowing.

As you know, Upchurch Station was a terminus, which meant it was the last station on the line; but just behind the station was the depot, where all the trains were put to bed at night.

When Derek wasn't out driving a train, he was always to be found pottering around the depot, helping out the depot staff with various odd jobs. One day, when he was doing just that, Fred the Foreman called to him.

"Hey, Derek, I've got some news for you." Derek ambled over to where Fred stood, just inside the office door. "What's up?" said Derek.

"It looks like Old 97 is going at last," said Fred, handing Derek a letter.

Derek's face fell as he read all the details. You see, Old 97 was the first engine that Derek had ever worked on when he started work all those years ago as a young cleaner, and he had become very fond of it.

Originally, Old 97 was the pride of the fleet, built in Queen Victoria's day, heading up all the important trains of the time, but now the engine stood cold and forlorn in the far corner of the engine shed.

As he read the letter, it told its own story. Old 97 had been sold, together with a large number of other old engines, to Cutter's Scrap Yard. Derek knew the place. Mr Cutter was not a sympathetic man when it came to steam engines.

His scrap yard was just outside Bigtown, where rows and rows of old engines stood, waiting their turn to be cut up for scrap.

Derek put down the letter and turned to the foreman.

"Could we light her up one last time - just for old times' sake?" he asked, fighting to hold back the tears he felt welling up inside.

The foreman's face softened and, putting his arm around Derek's shoulder, he said, "Aye, of course we can. We've got Old 97 for a few more days. Mind you, we can't really have a big fire in her and put her in steam - that old boiler wouldn't stand it."

"Never mind," said Derek, "just seeing a bit of smoke curling up from that old chimney again will be wonderful."

And so it was the very next day, the depot foreman was as good as his word and Derek, and all the other drivers, stood and watched smoke curling up from Old 97's chimney for the very last time, for in a couple of days Mr Cutter was coming to take the engine away on his big low loader lorry.

Even though it was nice to pretend Old 97 was in steam again, Derek wandered home that evening with a heavy heart.

As usual, he passed Sam the Signalman's little house and noticed Sam watering the flowers in his garden. Sam looked up and greeted Derek.

"Hi, there, mate!" he said. "Sorry to hear about Old 97 going."

"Never mind," said Derek, "I suppose it had to happen one day. How's Betsy?" he asked, changing the subject.

Betsy was Sam's ginger cat and she kept
Sam company when he came home after a
busy day in the signal box.

"Dunno," said Sam, "she's missing.
I haven't seen her for a couple of days.
She's been behaving a bit strangely lately.
I hope she hasn't got lost somewhere."

"No," said Derek, "I expect she'll turn up." The two men said farewell and Derek went home for his supper.

Soon the day arrived when Mr Cutter was to collect Old 97. All the depot staff, engine drivers and as many people who could be there, were there. They all wanted to say goodbye to Old 97.

The old engine had been gently hauled out to the loading dock, which would help Mr Cutter to lower his lorry ramp and load Old 97 aboard.

Mr Cutter duly arrived and set about attaching a winch to Old 97's buffer beam, so that he could haul it up the ramp and on to his lorry.

Derek pleaded with him not to take Old 97, but Mr Cutter was not a lover of steam engines.

"That's good scrap money!" he said, dismissing Derek's appeal with a wave of his hand.

Well, at last everything was ready and, inch by inch, the winch strained to pull the engine forward. Squeak, squeak, squeak went the winch. Jerk, jolt, jerk went the old engine.

Mr Cutter had the engine nearly halfway up the ramp, but decided to stop for a cup of tea. Squeak, squeak, squeak went the winch - or so they thought, but Sam the Signalman had noticed that the winch had stopped, so how could it still be squeaking? He tapped Mr Cutter on the shoulder.

"Hey, what's that noise?" he asked.

Mr Cutter stopped drinking his tea, and looked puzzled. Together, he and Sam inspected the winch and then the engine. Squeak, squeak, squeak, came the distinct sound.

"Quick," said Sam, "open the smokebox."

Now a smokebox is that part of an engine which the chimney comes out of at the front.

There are two levers that look like the hands of a clock, that usually keep the smokebox door locked, but Sam and Mr Cutter noticed the levers were undone. They swung open the smoke box door.

As they peered inside, they were amazed at what they saw. For curled up around the blast pipe was Sam the Signalman's ginger cat Betsy; and even more amazing, were six little ginger kittens.

Squeak, squeak, squeak, went the little kittens, as Betsy proudly washed them with her tongue, purring loudly.

Well, as you can imagine, there was great consternation. Betsy wasn't going to move for anybody. You see, steam engines stay warm for a very long time after the fire goes out and Betsy had sneaked into Old 97's open smokebox when no-one was looking and snuggled down in the warm, ready to give birth to her kittens.

Mr Cutter was perplexed, but Sam was a wise signalman, and he took Mr Cutter to one side for a chat. Then he went and spoke to Derek, and so it was all agreed.

You see, Mr Cutter didn't care much for steam engines, but he loved cats, and when Betsy made Old 97 her home, he didn't have the heart to disturb her.

"Derek," called Mr Cutter, "I've had a word with Sam, and we've agreed that when the time is right, the kittens will come to live with me, and keep my scrap yard free of rats.

"But in the meantime, Betsy mustn't be disturbed. That means Old 97 will be staying here. It seems Old 97 is a lucky engine, and I think it should be saved!"

This made Derek extremely happy.
In fact, everyone was extremely happy.
Mr Cutter got his kittens; Sam the Signalman got his Betsy back; and Derek had saved
Old 97 from the scrap yard.

Today, Old 97 stands at the front of the station, with a new coat of paint, gleaming in the sunshine, and a kind passerby has put a plaque on the buffer beam which says:

"Old 97, Rescued by Betsy."

OLD 97
RESCUED BY
BETSY

TALES OF
UPCHURCH STATION

STANLEY
THE STATIONMASTER
AND THE FESTIVAL

by Robert Gillman

As you know, Upchurch was one of those places where there could be great activity and then times when nothing much seemed to happen at all. This applied as much to the station as it did to the town.

"Very quiet, very quiet," muttered Stanley the Stationmaster, as he sat in his station office. All the morning rush hour trains had departed, and all his rushing around on the station, giving directions to passengers and instructions to drivers and guards, had finished.

So now he sat at his desk, fiddling with his pencil. He had dealt with all the incoming post and all the outgoing parcels, and he was getting bored.

"Quiet, very quiet," he muttered again. Suddenly, "Trinnnng!" went the 'phone.

Stanley nearly jumped out of his chair and into the pot of ink he kept for stamping important parcels!

He quickly composed himself and picked up the 'phone.

It was Sir Harry Hurry and, as Sir Harry Hurry was always in a hurry, Stanley was soon scribbling away with his pencil.

"Yes, Sir Harry! No, Sir Harry!"

"Good-bye, Sir Harry!" said Stanley, as he put the 'phone down.

You see, Sir Harry had just come from a meeting with the town council, where everything concerning Upchurch was decided upon; and something very important had been decided upon. It was this.

It was almost 100 years since the railway had come to Upchurch, and that event had really put the town on the map, bringing people and prosperity to the area. So it had been decided that there would be a Festival in the town to celebrate, and Stanley had been asked to come up with an idea for the station to play a part in the event.

Well, Stanley had no idea what to do, and the rest of that day he could be seen pacing up and down the platforms, scratching his head and muttering much more than usual.

Even by tea time he was none the wiser and went off home, still scratching his head.

Stanley lived at the other end of town.
He wasn't married, and lived on his own in
one of a little row of cottages. As he sat with
his feet up and a nice cup of tea, he continued
to puzzle as to what he could do for the
Festival.

Just then, there was a tap, tap, tap at the
door. It was Auntie Ivy. Now she wasn't his
real Auntie, but just the old lady who lived in
a house across the street.

"I thought you might like a bit of
cottage pie," said Ivy.

You see, Ivy was always being kind to folk and making homemade jam or pies and giving them to neighbours. She lived all alone with only her little dog Charlie for company, and sometimes she would feel very lonely.

"Thank you," said Stanley, taking the hot pie, which would do very nicely for his supper. "That's very kind."

"I can see you've just got in from work, so I'll leave you to it," said Ivy, and then she was gone. Stanley wished she wasn't so lonely, and could have as many friends as he had.

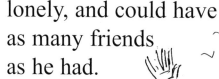

Stanley sat down and tucked into his delicious supper. He had just finished the last mouthful, when he had an idea!

Immediately he got on the 'phone to Sir Harry Hurry, and explained his idea.
Sir Harry thought it was an excellent one, and the very next day, Stanley started making plans.

After a few more days, he went and
knocked on Auntie Ivy's door, and went in for
a chat. Charlie came up and licked his hand
as he always did, and then sat down and
wagged his tail excitedly. Stanley then
proceeded to tell Ivy his plan, and this was it:

He explained to Ivy about the 100 year
Festival and that he wanted to bring the
generations of young and old together.
So he planned to have a children's party at
the station.

All the town's children would be there, and all the senior citizens would also be there, to serve the children with cakes, jellies and ice cream.

Stanley knew that, although Ivy was very independent, she would agree to help, as she was always helping her neighbours whenever she could.

So it was all agreed. The time soon passed and the great day came.

All the town was decorated with flags and bunting and the Mayor and Sir Harry Hurry were to be seen greeting all sorts of important visitors from neighbouring towns. Down at the station, all the spare engines had been decked out with flowers, and the station buildings were covered in streamers and banners, while a brass band played enthusiastically at the entrance hall.

Auntie Ivy had been asked to arrive at 4 o'clock for the children's party, and was quickly ushered into one of the large rooms in the main station building.

Stanley asked her to sit down at the party table, which had already been decorated with candles, balloons and party hats. A number of other elderly folk from the town soon joined her and they sat and chatted and made friends while waiting for the arrival of the children.

But Ivy and her new-found friends didn't know that Stanley had a surprise up his sleeve and had literally turned the tables on *them*! Because it had been secretly arranged that it would be the children who would be serving tea to Ivy, and not Ivy serving the children.

You see, on behalf of the town, Stanley wanted to say "Thank you" to Ivy, and to all the senior citizens that had made possible the prosperity and success of Upchurch.

They had been there in the early days and had helped the town become what it was today; and today the town was saying "Thank you."

Ivy had a wonderful time and got to know many of the town's children that lived nearby. When the party came to an end, she had made lots of new friends, and they all promised that they would visit each other often.

This was exactly the result Stanley had been hoping for, and he smiled contentedly, while Charlie just licked his hand, and wagged his tail.

Robert Gillman - Bob to his friends - grew up in East London, and ever since he can remember has loved trains, and steam trains in particular. At one time, his father was a boiler fitter's mate at the local Great Eastern Railway works at Stratford.

He has always been creative, and writes songs, poetry, and now children's stories.

With railways in his blood, he has been a volunteer fireman on the West Somerset Railway for over 15 years; he also works full time in the railway industry.

www.railway-cat.co.uk
email: railwaycat@clara.co.uk

Alan has spent most of his life in the West Country, particularly in the Bristol, Weston-super-Mare and Exmoor areas. He has painted all his life and has been a full time professional artist since 1985.

He is well-known for his Railway, Marine and Wildlife paintings, many of them commissions. A large number of these are published as fine art and limited edition prints. Several exhibitions are held throughout the year in various locations. For more information, or to contact Alan, please visit

www.alanwardcollection.co.uk
email: info@alanwardcollection.co.uk